GO EAT,
Pete

GO EAT, Pete

STORY BY
**GAIL M. NELSON
& KATIE NELSON**

ILLUSTRATED BY
GAIL M. NELSON

Printed in the United States of America

Katie Nelson & *Pete*

I dedicate this book to
all my friends.
KN

Pete's book is for all children
learning to make healthier choices.
GN

Gail M. Nelson
Mrs. Eatswell

What do you eat, Pete?

Monkeys munch on fruit.

Pete loves pizza.

Gorillas graze on greens.

What does Pete eat?

Mountain goats gorge on whole grains.

Pete gobbles up a cinnamon roll.

Wolves like lean meat.

What does Pete eat?

Elephants adore nuts and seeds.

Pete craves cotton candy.

Seals snack on seafood.

What does Pete eat?

Camels drink water.

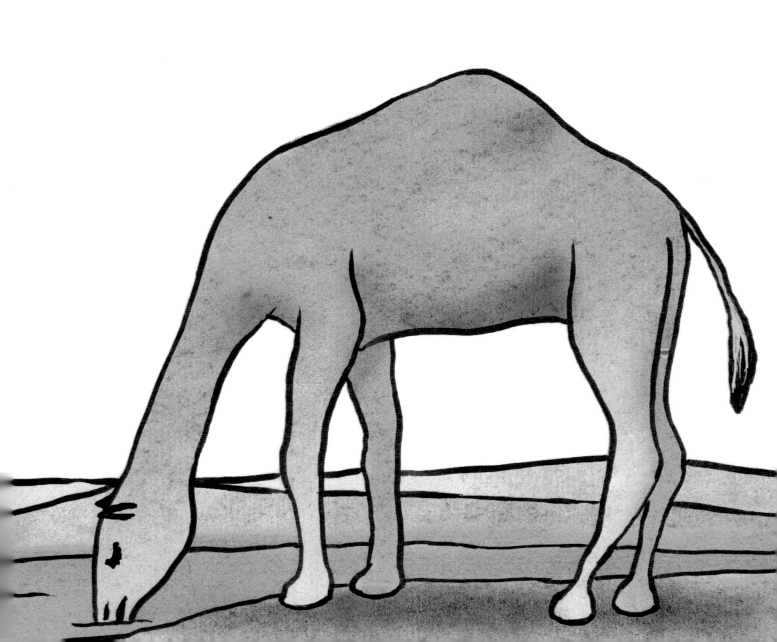

Pete slurps soda.

Cheetahs run fast,

Big Horn Sheep climb high,

and Sea Otters play.

Pete runs out of energy.

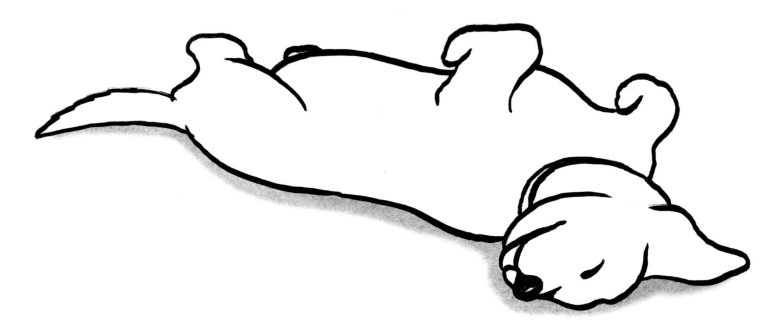

Whooo can make healthier choices?

Pete?

Discover a **rainbow** of healthier choices with Pete.

GO SLOW WHOA Foods

VEGETABLES & FRUITS

FISH

LEGUMES & BEANS

POULTRY

PROCESSED FOODS, SWEETS, TRANS FATS

EGGS

WHOLE GRAINS

BEEF & DAIRY

SEEDS & RAW NUTS

Made in the USA
Columbia, SC
01 April 2022